D0923049

SECRETS OF THE LIBRARY OF DOOM

THE HAUNTED HANDWRITING

BY MICHAEL DAHL
ILLUSTRATED BY PATRICIO CLAREY

STONE ARCH BOOKS
a capstone imprint

Published by Stone Arch Books, an imprint of Capstone
1710 Roe Crest Drive, North Mankato, Minnesota 56003
capstonepub.com

Library of Congress Cataloging-in-Publication Data
Names: Dahl, Michael, author. | Clarey, Patricio, 1978– illustrator. |
Dahl, Michael. Secrets of the library of doom.
Title: The haunted handwriting / by Michael Dahl ; illustrated by
Patricio Clarey.
Description: North Mankato, Minnesota : Stone Arch Books, an
imprint of Capstone, [2022] | Series: Secrets of the Library of
Doom | Audience: Ages 8–11. | Audience: Grades 4–6. | Summary:
In the dark, a detached human hand wearing a black ring seeks
someone to read the words of the magic spell it writes: a spell that
will bring the evil Dr. Merlinus back to life—and the Librarian
must act fast to prevent Merlinus from making a young boy his
next victim. Includes discussion questions.
Identifiers: LCCN 2021028483 (print) | LCCN 2021028484 (ebook)
| ISBN 9781663976734 (hardcover) | ISBN 9781666329810
(paperback) | ISBN 9781666329827 (pdf)
Subjects: LCSH: Librarians—Juvenile fiction. | Hand—Juvenile
fiction. | Incantations—Juvenile fiction. | Good and evil—
Juvenile fiction. | Horror tales. | CYAC: Librarians—Fiction. |
Hand—Fiction. | Magic—Fiction. | Good and evil—Fiction. |
Horror stories. | LCGFT: Horror fiction.
Classification: LCC PZ7.D15134 Haw 2022 (print) | LCC PZ7.
D15134 (ebook) | DDC 813.54 [Fic]—dc23
LC record available at https://lccn.loc.gov/2021028483
LC ebook record available at https://lccn.loc.gov/2021028484

Designed by Hilary Wacholz

TABLE OF CONTENTS

The Library of Doom is a hidden fortress.
It holds the world's largest collection
of strange and dangerous books.

Behold the Librarian. He defends the Library—and
the world—from super-villains, clever thieves,
and fierce monsters. Many of his adventures
have remained secret. Now they can be told.

SECRET #251

HANDBOOKS ARE NOT
ALWAYS HELPFUL.

Chapter One

THE HANDBOOK

A door slams shut on a small, **DARK** street.

A bookshop has just closed for the night.

NO one is left inside the shop. There are only books.

A faint noise comes from the back of the shop.

TAP. TAP. TAP.

The sound comes from an ancient book sitting on a table.

Earlier, a **STRANGE** man had walked into the store.

The man's hands were wrapped in bandages. He sold the **OLD** book.

The bookshop owner didn't have time
to put the book away on a shelf.

TAP. TAP. TAP.

The **ANCIENT** book has a title on
its cover.

The tapping stops.

The cover of the **ANCIENT** book moves. It opens barely an inch.

Out from under the cover **CRAWLS** a dark shape.

It is a hand.

The hand is **NOT** attached to a body.

Chapter Two

THE HAND AND THE RING

The hand is old and WRINKLED.

A silver ring gleams on its pointer finger. In the center of the ring is a stone as **BLACK** as ink.

The hand **JUMPS** off the table and crawls along the floor.

When the hand reaches the shop's front door, it stops.

Then it begins to **CLIMB** up the door.

The hand moves like an insect. Its fingers stick to the wood.

The hand **CRAWLS** until it reaches a small window above the door.

It opens the window.

SQUUUUUEEEEEAAKK!

The hand slips outside.

Slowly, the hand **MOVES** up the side of the building.

It **GRABS** onto the bricks and pulls itself up.

The hand makes NO noise as it climbs.

Then it **STOPS**.

Farther up the building, another window opens.

A young boy **LEANS** out of the window to get some fresh air.

This is what the hand was **HUNTING** for—a reader. The hand climbs toward the boy.

Chapter Three

IT CRAWLS

The young boy goes back to his bed.

The air inside the room is **WARM**.
So, he leaves the window wide open.

He does not hear the hand CRAWLING
outside.

Two WRINKLED fingers grab the window sill.

They pull **UP** the rest of the hand.

The hand sits quietly on the sill like a spider.

Then the hand moves again. It **FLOPS** onto the bedroom floor.

The hand quietly crawls farther into the room.

KRITCH-KRITCH-KRITCH-KRITCH

The boy does not hear the moving hand. He does not see it either. He lies with his face **TURNED** away from the window.

The hand stops in the middle of the floor.

The **BLACK** gem on its ring pops open. Ink begins to flow slowly from the ring.

The ink **OOZES** down the hand's pointer finger.

The black liquid **DRIPS** off the sharp fingernail.

The hand uses the ink to **WRITE** on the bare floor.

It writes **STRANGE** words and letters.

SCRATCH-SCRATCH SCRATCH-SCRATCH

The noise wakes the boy.

Chapter Four

GHOST WRITING

The boy is too afraid to **SHOUT**.

From his bed, he watches the hand write in a **WIDE** circle.

The boy tries to read the **STRANGE** words.

He does not understand the words,
but he quietly sounds them out.

"Guh-thool-ooh-grak-grak-hoomla."

Suddenly, the handwriting **WIGGLES**
like black worms on the floor.

The boy wants to run out of his room.
But the wiggling **WRITING** is between
him and the door.

The hand stops writing. It sits in the circle of moving words.

A **BLACK** hole opens up inside the circle.

The hand begins to **RISE** above the hole.

Something HORRIBLE comes with it.

The hand is now attached to a pale white arm.

Then the boy sees a **GHOSTLY** head, neck, and shoulders rise up into his bedroom.

Soon, a **STRANGE** pale man floats above the floor.

He is wearing a coat with black **GEMS**. The silver ring gleams on his right hand.

"Behold, you have brought Dr. Merlinus back to life," says the man. "Now you shall become part of my story forever!"

Chapter Five

WHOSE STORY?

The boy feels COLD.

He looks down. The wiggling words are **CRAWLING** onto his feet.

"Get off me!" shouts the boy. "Somebody help!"

FRRRROOOOOOSHH-SHHH!

The boy hears a loud rushing sound above him.

A second hole has appeared on the ceiling. This one is blue.

The boy sees boots coming **DOWN** from the hole.

Then a man appears. He is wearing a long coat and **DARK** glasses.

That looks like the Librarian from my books! thinks the boy.

"Help me!" the boy **CRIES** to the hero.

The Librarian points at the pale ghost. "Why are you here, Merlinus? You were **BANISHED** from Earth!" he says.

"But my writing stayed behind," says the ghost. "When others read my story and bring it to life, then I live too."

"Everyone has their *own* story," says the Librarian. "And yours has reached The End."

The Librarian takes a **SHINING** pen from his coat.

He **THROWS** it onto the floor.

The pen **WRITES** new words.

They cover the haunted handwriting.

The inky black **HOLE** on the floor grows smaller and smaller.

The ghost **SCREAMS** as he turns to smoke and blows away.

The silver ring falls onto the floor.

PING!

The Librarian scoops up the ring.
He hands it to the boy.

"Is it still magic?" asks the boy.

The Librarian SHAKES his head.

"No," says the hero. "But if you visit
the bookshop below, you'll find magic
in every book you open."

GLOSSARY

ancient (EYN-shunt)—extremely old

attached (uh-TACHD)—connected to something

bandage (BAN-dij)—a strip of cloth that is wrapped around a hurt body part to protect it

banish (BAN-ish)—to send far away as a punishment

faint (FEYNT)—so weak or unclear that it is hard to hear, see, taste, or feel

gleam (GLEEM)—to shine brightly

handbook (HAND-book)—a book of information on a subject that often has steps on how to do something, such as fixing a car or going camping (or casting magic spells!)

haunted (HAWN-ted)—affected or visited often by a ghost

liquid (LIK-wid)—any wet substance that flows like water

scoop (SKOOP)—to lift up

TALK ABOUT IT

1. In this tale, a ghost tries to return to Earth. Have you read any other stories with ghosts? How are they similar to this story? How are they different?

2. How do you think the boy felt when the Librarian came down from the hole in his bedroom ceiling? What makes you think that?

WRITE ABOUT IT

1. At the end of the story, the Librarian says, "You'll find magic in every book you open." Write a paragraph explaining what you thinks this means.

2. *The Handbook of Dr. Merlinus* is still in the bookshop. Will anything else crawl out of the ancient book? Write a new story about what happens next!

ABOUT THE AUTHOR

Michael Dahl is an award-winning author of more than 200 books for young people. He especially likes to write scary or weird fiction. His latest series are the sci-fi adventure Escape from Planet Alcatraz and School Bus of Horrors. As a child, Michael spent lots of time in libraries. "The creepier, the better," he says. These days, besides writing, he likes traveling and hunting for the one, true door that leads to the Library of Doom.

ABOUT THE ILLUSTRATOR

Patricio Clarey was born in Argentina. He graduated in fine arts from the Martín A. Malharro School of Visual Arts, specializing in illustration and graphic design. Patricio currently lives in Barcelona, Spain, where he works as a freelance graphic designer and illustrator. He has created several comics and graphic novels, and his work has been featured in